For Susan, Ben and Eva – and all the rabbits at Marden Hill – C.L.
For Bunny Rabbit, with love X X X – S.A.

Series concept and design: Liz Black
Book design: Jane Hawkins
Commissioning Editor: Lisa Edwards
Editor: Katie Orchard
Science Consultant: Dr Carol Ballard

Published in Great Britain in 2002 by Hodder Wayland,
an imprint of Hodder Children's Books

Cataloguing in publication data
Llewellyn, Claire
    The Best Ears in the World: A first look at sound and hearing. – (Little Bees)
    1. Hearing – pictorial works – Juvenile literature 2. Ear – pictorial works –
    Juvenile literature 3. Sound – pictorial works – Juvenile literature
    I. Title
    612.8'5 [J]

ISBN 07502 3799 6

Printed and bound in Grafiasa, Porto, Portugal

Hodder Children's Books
A division of Hodder Headline Limited
338 Euston Road, London NW1 3BH

The Best Ears in the World

A first look at sound and hearing

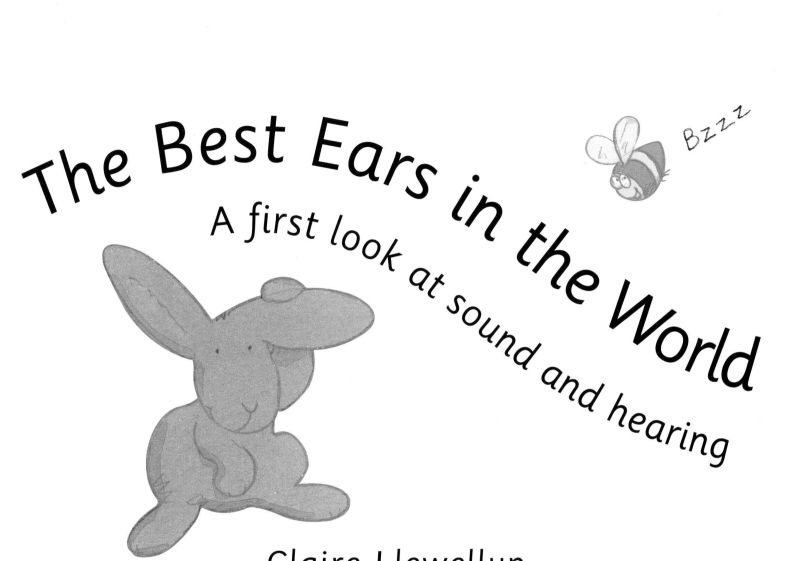

The Best Ears in the World
A first look at sound and hearing

Claire Llewellyn

HODDER
Wayland

an imprint of Hodder Children's Books

It is early morning. A little rabbit is

Dad, why do rabbits have such silly ears?

6

looking at himself in the pond.

Our ears aren't silly, son! They're very important.

I think we're going to find out why.

The rabbits make their way along the lane.

They greet the horses in the field.

Suddenly there's an angry gabbling.

The rabbits scamper away.

What's that noise, Dad?

It's the geese, son. They sound grumpy. Let's keep out of their way!

The rabbits stop to catch their breath,

Because he's singing. Most things move when they make a sound.

and listen to a blackbird's song.

13

All at once, there's a *rat-a-tat!*

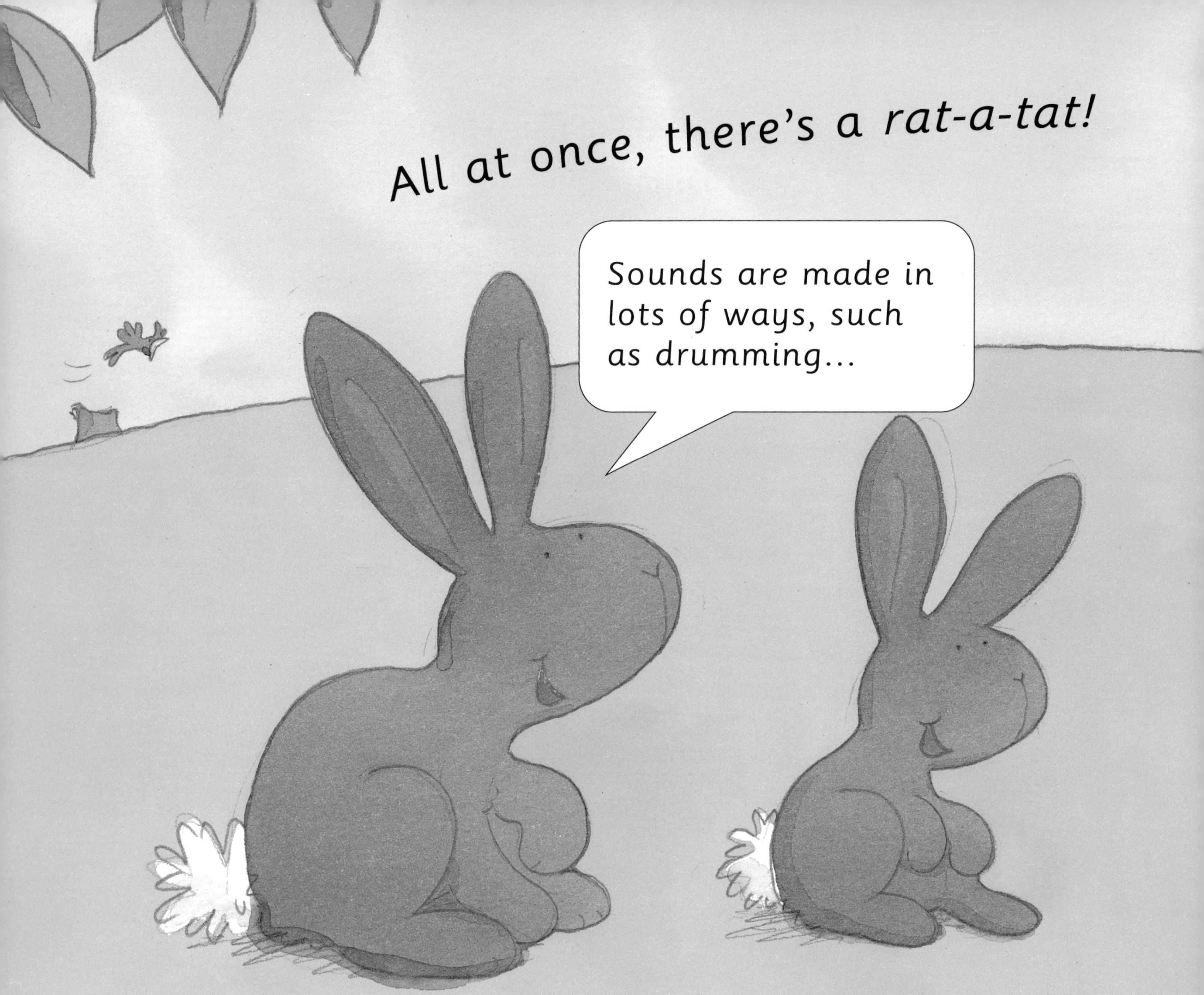

A woodpecker is drumming on a tree.

… and plucking…

… and shaking…

… and blowing!

Something is coming up the hill.

It's the farmer's noisy tractor.

and slowly moves away.

Everything is quiet and still.

I can hear the buzz of a bumble bee.

Bzzz

You've got very sharp ears!

Now, as the light begins to fade,

I can't hear anything.

the rabbits turn for home.

Suddenly a barn owl swoops.

The rabbits dive for cover.

The rabbits are about to cross a road

when a car roars into view.

The rabbits are in their burrow at last.

And do you still think our ears are silly, son?

They are cosy, safe and warm.

No, Dad. They're not silly. They're the best ears in the world!

All about sounds and hearing

Our ears help
us to hear.

Our ears tell us where
a sound is coming from.

Very loud sounds can
hurt our ears.

There are many
different ways of
making sounds.

Most things move when they make a sound.

Sounds seem louder, the nearer we are to them.

Sounds seem quieter, the further we are from them.

Useful Words

Blowing
Puffing air.

Drumming
Tapping or banging.

Plucking
Pulling an object with your finger.

Wobbling
Moving something to and fro very quickly.